WE **CAN**
ONLY
HOPE
FOR **IT**

OTHER NOVELS BY HARRY KATZAN, JR.
A Matt and the General Series

Life is Good

Everything is Good

The Last Adventure

The Romeo Affair

Another Romeo Affair

*****

WE **CAN** ONLY HOPE FOR **IT**

Harry Katzan Jr.

WE CAN ONLY HOPE FOR IT

iUniverse books may be ordered through booksellers or by contacting:

iUniverse
1663 Liberty Drive
Bloomington, IN 47403
www.iuniverse.com
844-349-9409

Because of the dynamic nature of the Internet, any web addresses or links contained in this book may have changed since publication and may no longer be valid. The views expressed in this work are solely those of the author and do not necessarily reflect the views of the publisher, and the publisher hereby disclaims any responsibility for them.

Any people depicted in stock imagery provided by Getty Images are models, and such images are being used for illustrative purposes only. Certain stock imagery © Getty Images.

ISBN: 978-1-6632-5360-6 (sc)
ISBN: 978-1-6632-5362-0 (hc)
ISBN: 978-1-6632-5361-3 (e)

Library of Congress Control Number: 2023910042

Print information available on the last page.

iUniverse rev. date: 06/02/2023

For Margaret, my best girl now and forever

with all my love

and Kathryn and Karen

Contents

Part 4: The Plot Thickens

Part 5: The Search for a Solution

Part 6: Back to Normal

Introduction

This novel, as in the previous fifteen stories in the series involving Matt and the General, with the assistance of their associates and friends, Matt and the General combine their efforts to solve important problems that involve the safety of the United States, along with problems in the domestic arena. In this instance. the book is set in the beautiful area of middle New Jersey, the United States in general, and in several foreign countries.

As in the previous novels, Matt Miller, who has a PhD degree from a prestigious university, and uses mathematical thinking and solid logic, along with the organizational ability of General Les Miller, his grandfather, to solve several major problems, recognized by the President and the Intelligence Director of the United States, as well as two local problems that require the wisdom of the team. The subject matter is supplanted with a historical sequence that described the origin of the General and other team members, by way of three introductory chapters that are interesting in their own right.

In this set of episodes, the General is called back to regular duty and only plays a minor role the episode. Matt, Ashley, and Matt's university friend Harp Thomas share the responsibility for investigating a very unusual situation. You will be surprised and perhaps even determining that the problem is a problem.

The ideas herein change rapidly, but always in the scope of no violence, no sex, and no bad language. The book typifies the conventional "beach" read in that the subject matter can be read as five separate stories.

This is the sixteenth book in the Matt and the General series. The characters assume their dynamic personalities as in previous tales.

The Author,
June, 2023

Main Characters in the Book

The General – Les Miller. Former military General and Humanitarian. P-51 pilot and World War II hero.

Matthew (Matt) Miller – Professor of Mathematics. Grandson of the General. Sophisticated problem solver and strategist.

Ashley Wilson Miller – College friend of Matt Miller. Former Duchess of Bordeaux. Married to Matt Miller. Is a Receiver of the National Medal of Freedom.

Marguerite Purgoine - Retired creative writing Professor and an associate of the team. Known as Anna for some unknown reason. Wife of the General.

General Clark - Mark Clark. Former Four Star General and Chairman of the Joint Chiefs of Staff. Appointed to be U.S. Director of Intelligence.

Kimberly Scott – The Intelligence specialist of the U.S.

Harry Steevens – Expert mathematician and former college friend of Matt Miller. Policeman in New Jersey.

Katherine Penelope Radford – Retired Queen of the United Kingdom and personal friend of the General.

Harp Thomas – Academic friend of Matt and professor of mathematics at ETH Zürich Switzerland.

Gregory Kacan – Matt's and Harp's thesis advisor. Retired professor.

Katarina Kacan – Gregory's wife. Deceased in the story.

Harry Steevens – Friend of Matt's and law enforcement officer.

Dr. Hutchinson - Military psychiatrist and project leader.

END OF CHARACTERS

Part 1

CHARACTERS IN THE STORY

Chapter 1

LIFE IS GOOD

It was a good golfing day in New Jersey. The sky was a deep blue without a cloud and there was a nip of coolness in the air. There was a slight breeze, and the deciduous trees that were losing their leaves were moving in unison. It was a Monday, and it seemed that if something were going to happen, it would happen on Monday. Matthew Miller, known as Matt practically everywhere, was a professor of mathematics at a prestigious university. He had his PhD degree that he had earned in only two years. He was an acknowledged scholar, and it was genuinely thought that he knew everything there was to know about mathematics. He had an academic relationship with fellow mathematicians all over the world.

On this particular Monday Matt had two classes, a graduate math class at 9:00 am and an undergrad math class at 10:00 am, followed by a meeting with his PhD candidate at 11:00 am. Then to top it off, he had a last minute departmental meeting at 1:00 pm. The General wanted to play a round of golf, so they scheduled it at 3:00 pm at the local Country Club of which Matt and his grandfather, known as the General, were members. Matt's classes went well, as they always did. For each class, the students had to do a problem set due the next class. Each submission was evaluated by a teaching assistant and given a value of 1 through 5. Matt graded his own exams, since he was interested in how well his lectures were preparing the students for exams. Matt loved his classes, and his students liked him, usually because he had a gentleman's attitude toward them. Matt was very supportive of his PhD candidate. Each semester, he had one grad course and one undergrad course and at least one PhD candidate to advise. As such, he was a math professor, and that was what he wanted to be. He was a full professor with tenure.

Matt's life was relatively simple. He prepared his lectures, played golf with the General, studied math to keep abreast of new things, and did things with his wife Ashley, who was a professor at a local community college. Matt and Ashley usually hung out together, including time at the local driving range. They normally did not play together on golf courses, since Matt and the General were expert players, and Matt had been an NCAA golf champion.

The General is a retired Army Air Force 3-star general officer and had received a retired fourth star, so he had the rank of a 4-star general. A general is a general for life, so the General kept his ties to the active military world. Les Miller, the General, was a former P-51 pilot, as well as a B-29 and B-52 pilot, and had performed several honorable deeds, so he was usually known socially as the General.

The General has bachelors, masters, and doctorate degrees, and was the founder of a political polling company that had made him a very wealthy man, who chose to use his wealth to help people. Matt and the General have completed several goodwill projects together.

At 1:00 pm, the math department Chairman had an unscheduled departmental meeting, to which the Dean and the department's secretary were also invited. The department Chairman started the meeting, "Greetings everyone, and welcome to our guest Dean Fletcher. We are here to honor one of our colleagues, who is designated by the Board of Directors of the university as a Distinguished Scholar. Therefore, I would like to honor Matthew Miller with that award. He will receive a certificate, a staff assistant to assist in performing his research, a substantial raise in salary, and a reduced teaching load of one course."

The people in the room clapped, and each member of the faculty gave an elegant fountain pen to Dr. Miller. A professor in the back of the room wondered where all of those beautiful fountain pens came from and finally realized that the university maintained several sets for future awards. In the celebrated movie *A Beautiful Mind*, a roomful of guests gave pens to the celebrated mathematician John Nash for winning the Nobel Prize in which a larger number of fountain pens changed hands.

Matt replied, "Thank you for the honor and the handsome set of fountain pens. I definitely feel humbled at this award. However, I do have one brief question. Am I expected to teach only one course?"

"That would normally be the case," replied the Chairman.

"If I cannot teach one grad course and one undergrad course, I will deny the award," stated Matt.

The Chairman looked at the Dean, who smiled as if to say 'I told you so' or 'It's your problem'. "Then it is in my power to

3

assign the normal load to Dr. Miller," said the chairman. All of the members of the department clapped, and all shook Matt's hand. A light lunch was served.

Matt was completely dismayed by the entire state of affairs with the university, in particular, and the whole education system, in general. *Teaching math is a distinct pleasure,* Matt thought, *and as the courses get harder, only the good students go on. So the courses are more enjoyable. I'm kind of proud of myself for sticking up to my rights in education during the ceremony.*

Matt headed home, changed clothes, tossed his clubs into the back of his sports car headed to the Country Club.

When Matt got to the Country Club, the General was in a jubilant mood and initiated the conversation with a big smile. "Hi Matt, how has your day been so far?"

Matt had a scowl on his face, so the General immediately knew that something was amiss.

"It was good and bad," said Matt. "My classes went well. They always do. I like the students. The PhD candidate has made good progress on his dissertation, since he finished his course work and passed his comprehensive exam. It's what happened afterwards that has put me in a bad mood, and you know that I'm almost never in a bad mood."

"Tell me about it," said the General. "I'm sure we can fix anything that has gone wrong."

"They gave me a distinguished professor award," said Matt. "It's one of those things that the Board of Directors does. The award includes a certificate, a raise in salary, an assistant, and a reduced workload to only one course per semester."

"Doesn't sound too bad to me," said the General.

"I like my courses, one grad, one undergrad, and a PhD candidate to advise, so I said that if I could only teach one course, then I would deny the award. So the math department Chairman, who has changed, looked at the Dean who smiled, as if to say 'It's your problem' or 'I told you so'. So the Chairman graciously said he would work it out, and I could carry my usual course load. Everyone clapped, and each professor in the department gave me an elegant fountain pen and a handshake. It's a tradition."

I knew about it," said the General. "I knew that was how you would respond."

"You knew about it?" replied Matt.

"The Dean invited me," answered the General. "I know him from our military days. I turned down the invite, because I thought something like that would happen. You're not the only one that can figure things out."

"Well, I'll be," said Matt. "I think I'm going to enjoy our round of golf."

Matt was right. He and the General both played their best round in a couple of years. Afterwards, the General invited Matt and Ashley to have dinner with Mme. Purgoine, the prize winning author and retired professor of creative writing, and himself at the Green Room, the prize winning restaurant that he owned.

Matt accepted without asking Ashley, since he knew she always enjoyed a fine dinner in a classy restaurant. Matt recognized that the General was more enthusiastic about the dinner than normal, so he knew something was up, and it wasn't about the distinguished professor award.

Ashley returned from a college at which she also was a professor, and was very pleased about the dinner. She even wore an appropriate dress and spiked heel shoes, even though she knew a dress and heels was less popular in the modern world. Matt was proud that Ashley knew how to dress for an occasion. Most modern women dressed in trousers and flats in some ridiculous new fashion.

At the dinner seated at the best table in the house, the General told about Matt's award, and the ladies were proud of their favorite person. The General told about Matt's desire to keep his usual schedule and they just nodded, not getting the gist of the situation.

Then, the general announced his surprise, "I checked into your schedules and know that we now have time to do something interesting. I hereby propose that the four of us take a short vacation at the best hotel in Maui. We'll take the Gulfstream 650 that has been retrofitted with high performance fan jet engines and long distance fuel tanks. I checked on the airport situation, and we can land at the commercial airfield."

"Our pilots have changed slightly," said the General. "The older one wanted to spend more time with family, so we recruited a new one, who was also an F-22 Raptor pilot. So the first officer will be the Captain and the new pilot will be the First Officer."

The General looked up, and, he saw three of the biggest smiles that he had ever seen.

Matt asked about golf, and the General said that Maui had the best courses in Hawaii. Ashley asked about transportation, and the General said that he had arranged for a limo from a rental agency owned by a fellow officer. Mme. Purgoine, the General's wife, who went by the nickname Anna for some unknown reason, asked about shopping and entertainment, and the General said that the hotel had an entertainment package that consisted of a shopping spree, a luau, and an airplane flight over the site of the World War II attack by the Japanese, and a choice of 14 golf courses. He added that in all of Hawaii there were 75 courses.

All that Matt could say was, "General, you are the best planner that anyone could want."

The general and his entourage agreed that it was the best dinner ever.

During the dinner, a couple at another table stared at the four friends incessantly. The lady was heard to say, "Those people are so friendly and are having such a good time, I wonder why." Her husband responded, "They're Americans, and America is the world's best place to live."

And this is the way it was.

END OF CHAPTER ONE

Chapter 2

TRAVEL TO MAUI AND WASHINGTON

The General finalized the arrangements to use the Gulfstream 650 for the trip to Maui that he had mentioned. He contacted the pilot team that consisted of the two former F-22 Raptor pilots, and they were pleased with the extended range afforded by the new engines and additional fuel tanks. The 650 had a range of 7000 miles at 600 miles per hour flying at 51,000 feet. The distance to Maui is roughly 4,500 miles, well within the capacity of the aircraft. For experienced pilots, a nine-hour flight is certainly within the human endurance limit. However, he wondered about Matt, Ashley, and Anna. Matt recommended a non-stop flight, so the General decided to go ahead and make it a direct flight. The pilots were pleased with landing at a commercial airfield, and the car rental would be a breeze. The General was looking forward to using a Cadillac Escalade that he had ordered as a rental car.

The General's only open item were the golf clubs, and Matt said he didn't want to lug his expensive set of clubs in and out of an aircraft. The General called his military buddy, who was the car dealer, and he had a solution that entailed having two sets made. He said, "Just give me your measurement and club weights, and I'll have them in the Escalade when you get here." Matt knew his specifications, but the General had to go to the golf pro at the Country Club to be measured. Actually, the club pro used the General's everyday clubs and took the measurement from them.

From previous experience, the General knew the west shore of Maui in the Kaanapali area was the best for their needs. He choose a luxurious hotel with extensive facilities near a golf course. The hotel had a weekly luau, which is a wonderful eating experience.

Each of the guests asked about what to pack, and each got the same reply. "Travel light. Wear street clothes and extras for the first night. Otherwise, you can buy anything you need or want at my expense. This trip is my reward to you for helping to make our lives enjoyable and fulfilling."

The General scheduled the trip from Sunday to Thursday, with a few days just in case. They would leave New Jersey at 9:00 am and arrive at the Maui Air Base at 1:00 pm local time on the travel day to enjoy some tourism.

The Gulfstream took off on time, heading west. At about the same time, the Strategic Air Command in Nebraska received information that Air Force One would be traveling west. The commander at Dulles Air Base in Washington, DC emphasized that Air Force One did not need an escort, as was the White House custom. The Air Force One airplane had enough facilities and capability to protect itself. At the same time, he was informed that a Gulfstream 650 would also be heading west and be in Nebraska at about the same time. The identifier of the Gulfstream was traced to the General identified as the commander, along with his military rank.

The Gulfstream was being tracked by military radar, and it was determined that there were some anomalies. The Gulfstream was flying at 50,000 feet and traveling at 600 miles per hour. Because of Air Force One, the local base commander scrambled two F-22 Raptors because of the speed of the Gulfstream. The Air Force pilots were ordered to investigate the Gulfstream. The military Raptor pilot radioed the Gulfstream, and the Gulfstream Captain asked the Raptor pilot why they were tailing him. At this point, one F-22 was 10 miles from the Gulfstream and the other was 5. Not exactly a dangerous situation. The Raptor mentioned that Air Force One was only 20 miles away and the commander got jittery.

"It was determined that the Gulfstream pilots were former Raptor pilots and they had trained together," said the Captain. "The conversation took place at a distance of 5 miles, and finally got around to why the Gulfstream was being tailed in the first place. The presence of Air Force One that was 20 miles away was the reason. The Raptors returned to base, and the episode was complete. The First Officer went back to the passenger compartment and informed the General. The General mentioned the incident to Matt, who wondered where Air Force One could be going on a Sunday afternoon. The incident was humorous and lasted about 5 minutes."

The First Officer said he hadn't heard anything. The military pilot just doing his job. It happened all the time.

"Well, the President in Air Force One was heading west to be with a dying former associate," continued the Captain when he later described the situation. "He returned that night, as he always returned the same day as was his custom. He got back to the White House late and slept in the guest room as his wife had a bad case of the flu and he didn't want to wake her. He had a very busy schedule and did not get upstairs until late in the day. His wife wasn't there, and Secret Service said they had no idea of where she was. Someone mentioned that she probably went to see her mother in Ohio, and she would return soon. The agent said he would check on it. The President said that he was busy with some security issues and would follow up on it when he had a chance. Finally, they determined that nobody anywhere seemed to know where she was and the President went into a panic. That's what I heard anyway."

The Gulfstream arrived in Maui without any more surprises. and the four travelers had a Cadillac Escalade waiting for them, with a full tank of gas and two sets of golf clubs.

The vacation, if you wanted to call it that, was a total success. Matt and the General played four rounds of golf, and the luau and air excursion were enjoyable and definitely memorable. The ladies each bought a caftan called a muumuu at Hilo Hattie's shop, known for its vacation apparel. The men bought Hawaiian shirts, as men visiting Hawaii normally do. All got a terrific suntan, aided by advice from personnel in the hotel. After a few days of total relaxation, the team headed home.

The travelers were joyful after such a pleasant time. The special sets of golf clubs were gifts from the golf pro, and both Matt and the General decided to keep their sets. The trip home did not have a dreaded component to it, such as going back to work after a vacation, so everyone was free to discuss what they were going to do when they got home. As would be expected, Matt and the General agreed to hit the Country Club golf course at least 3 times a week, including weekends. Both were making their best golfing scores in Maui. Anna was going to sleep, and Ashley was going to work on her forthcoming textbook.

The real story of the White House adventure was a bit more detailed. Back in the contiguous United States, at about the same time that Matt, the General, Ashley, and Anna were leaving for Maui, Air Force One was readied in a hurry, the pilots were rounded up; the President and the Vice President, along with a minimal service staff, were on board, and the specially designed Boeing 747 airplane was headed to California in a hurry. Having the President and Vice President on the same flight caused some concern with the Secret Service, who were overruled by the President. The plane headed to San Jose at the maximum speed of 600 miles per hour at 40,000 feet. The President's life-long friend and former Chief of Staff was dying and the President and his friend had made a pact to be at the others bedside if death were imminent. The friend was dying of liver disease and wasn't expected to last the day. A few hours after the President arrived, the friend passed away, and Air Force One headed back to Washington. The President always returned home to the White House every night. He never slept away from his residence. Of course, there were exceptions for international trips.

When the President arrived back at the White House, it was late and he retired to a separate room in the presidential suite. He didn't want to wake the First Lady, who was nursing a bad case of the flu. Here is what supposedly happened.

The next morning, the President awakened early to read the

President's Daily Brief (PDB) and learned that the First Lady was not there. The President, who was used to having everything being well organized, went into panic mode and called the Secret Service. The President also called his trusted advisors to an urgent secret meeting in the blue room of the White House. The instructions were: (1) Find the First Lady, and (2) Keep the search a total secret from everyone. No one is to know in the U.S. or in the outside world. The logic was that the Americans people would be in a panic, the stock market would take a nose dive, and the news media would turn the situation into a frenzy. Several agencies would take care of the search and not tell anyone exactly why they were doing what they were doing. The known agencies were the FBI, CIA, NSA, Police Departments, Military Intelligence, and special units from the Marines and the Army. The Chairman of the Joint Chiefs of Staff, Mark Clark, a four star general, was consulted in total secrecy. In less than a week of search, there was no success.

Clark was optimistic. "We have persons in this country that operate under cover and who can solve practically any type of problem you can imagine." Clark continued in his advice to the President, "If they are available, I'll have them in your office in 24 hours."

The President was pleased. He liked Clark. If anyone could solve the problem, then it would be Clark.

General Clark called the General in New Jersey on his satellite phone and caught him asleep. "Les, we have a big problem here in DC, and I'm calling to see if you and Matt are available for a short consulting job. I agreed not to mention it over the wire, but it could be the biggest problem this country has had in a while. Are you and Matt available for a pick up at 9:00 am?"

"Okay, Mark," said the General, "Schedule a 9:00 pick up

and I'll inform Matt," said the General. "He's the most agreeable person on Earth, and I'm quite certain that he will agree. Maybe you don't know it, but he thinks you are the greatest general, and so do I. Do you know where to land here?"

"I don't," said Clark, "but the pilots do. I have to run."

The General called Matt, who had just turned on the coffee pot. "Matt, something big, real big is happening, and we have been summoned to the White House. Can you be ready for a 9:00 am pickup."

"If you can be ready, then I can be ready. I hope you are driving."

"I am, and I will pick you up at 8:45 at the latest," answered the General.

The White House jet landed exactly at 9:00 am and Matt and the General were waiting. Both had a small brief case but no luggage. Matt and the General knew the pilots from other White House problems.

"What took you so long?" asked the General.

"The Captain replied, "We're just slow people, General. Good morning."

"Good morning," replied the General. "I suspect that you don't know what is going on."

"Not a word," said the Captain. "Jump in, we're late."

The flight was smooth and fast. Commercial air traffic was averted for their flight, reflected in their flight plan, so the trip was as fast as they could possibly make it. A Marine One was waiting with its rotors turning. They landed on the White House lawn, and Matt and the General were escorted to the President's private office.

General Clark and Kenneth L Strong, the President, were waiting, having tracked the flight of Matt and the General on their electronic scoreboard.

<<<<<<<<<<<<<<<<<<<<<<

"Mr. President, I would like to introduce Matt and the General, about whom I spoke," said General Clark. "Gentlemen, this is President Strong."

"Welcome," said the President. "We have a big problem that I will describe to you. We hope you can help us with it."

The General replied," We are at your service Mr. President. We don't know the problem, yet. But I assure you that if it can be solved, and we can solve it."

"I hope you can," said the President.

"It will probably be straightforward, Sir," said Matt. "We have a set of axioms that we can use to prove something. In this case, please tell us, in detail, the problem, and there is a very high probability that we can solve it. But, just like in mathematics, some theorems can't be proved. But, then there is another theorem proving that all problems cannot be solved."

"Well, I certainly hope you can gentlemen. I will call in

George Benson, my go-to assistant. He has been spearheading the problem so far."

The President pressed a button on his desk, and spoke the name George Benson. In a few seconds, a non-descript middle-aged gentleman was ushered in

The President said, "Gentlemen, this is George Benson. He will be in charge of the problem solution. Meanwhile, I have a scheduled appointment with security council."

The President left through his private exit.

And this the way it was.

END OF CHAPTER TWO

Chapter 3

MATT AND THE GENERAL SHOW THEIR ABILITY

George Benson spoke first, "My name is George Benson. The President has asked me to solve a problem of a secret nature. I have worked for him for more than twenty years."

The General, Matt, and General Clark introduced themselves.

"I will outline what we have accomplished after I delineate the problem," said Benson. It was clear that he was used to stressful situations. "The problem is that the President returned from a quick trip to California and, as the hour was late, slept in the extra bedroom in the Presidential Suite. The President returns to the White House or other residence every night that he is out of town. The First Lady had been nursing a bad case of the flu, and the President did not want to disturb her. Upon wakening early the next morning to read the President's Daily Brief, the First Lady and her Secret Service escort were not in either the suite or the White House. The President always arises at 6:30 to read the PDB."

"The president instigated an alert and had an impromptu meeting with his staff," continued Benson. "He wanted his wife found, and he wanted no publicity of any kind. The secrecy is absolute. The FBI, CIA, NSA, Military Intelligence, and local Police were summoned and ordered to respond in total secrecy. A release of information would create a panic among the American people. Even the military were put on alert. You haven't heard of it because of the secrecy restriction. So far we have checked the White House thoroughly, which was a monumental task. There has been no sign of her. We have checked every means of travel including airports, train stations, automobile routes via toll stations, border patrol, hotels, and business establishments – legal and illegal. All of this was performed in total secrecy. The President thinks it might be a form of kidnapping, even though the FBI has said there is no evidence of that. There is no avenue that we have not explored. We have even checked the tunnel from the White House to the bunker beneath the Treasury Building. They came up with nothing there. Now the President is concerned about foreign adversaries, so the President has said we will have to go public fairly soon if she is not located."

"We can solve your problem," said Matt. "First, let me tell you a story. It will demonstrate how I – perhaps, I should say we – can and will solve the problem."

The General whispered to Mark Clark, "I surely hope he knows what he is doing."

"He does," replied Marl Clark, 4-star general, and Chief of the Joint Chiefs of Staff. "Look at his eyes and the way he talks. After

30 years in the Army, I can practically read a person's mind, and so can you. You're just out of practice, Les."

"Let me give an example of the approach that we can use," continued Matt. "It is an example of an analytic endeavor that actually took place."

Matt continued. "During World War II, the most advanced fighter plane was the American P-51, the aircraft of choice for American and English operations. One of the 'go to guys' for the P-51 is here today: General Les Miller, who we call General. He had finished with his deployment and was waiting for a new assignment. It's terrible to hear that 60% of the P-51s were shot down or destroyed in any one air raid. Let me emphasize that only 40% survived. The Army Air Force decided to apply titanium armor plates on the P-51s for protection, but that changed nothing. The developers inspected returning planes and patched areas that had bullet holes. It didn't work, so they decided to hold a conference on the subject and selected the General and Sir Charles Bunday, called Buzz, his wing-man, to attend. The conference was in Washington. The other attendees were professors, industrial mathematicians, and higher-ranking officers from Majors to Generals. The problem and the poor results were described to the attendees. This was a big deal conference, since the P-51 problem had been going on for some time."

Matt continued again. "After the problem was presented, Miller exclaimed that they were armor plating the wrong areas. He said they should use *reverse mathematics*. The other attendees laughed, how could two guys, who were only Captains, solve a problem that professors and senior Officers could not solve. Miller responded that they were looking at the wrong place. When a P-51 landed with bullet holes in a wing, they plated the wing with no change in results. He said that should be looking for areas that had no bullet holes, meaning that was why they were shot down. The solution, once you heard it, was obvious, and accepted by the central command. The number of planes shot down in any one raid was reduced to 10%. That is the kind of thinking we will use. It is called *Reverse Mathematics.*"

"We will use it on your problem," said Matt. "Here is how we should approach the problem of the First Lady. Your team from the FBI, CIA, and so forth, as good as they are, are going after the First Lady by looking in places she could be. They should be looking where she shouldn't or wouldn't be. So the question is, what are the places where she shouldn't be, and I guarantee there will not be too many of them around. So I would like a tour, together with the General, of the total scene of investigation."

So they started on a tour of the entire scene, not a crime scene, since no crime had been committed. The group toured every office in the White House and checked all of the private exits. They looked at the attic and all of the secret little rooms that are too small to be recognized ordinarily. The White House architect, many years earlier, had recorded none of his plans, nor did the builder, who didn't seem use any plans at all. Some say it was for security. They toured the bunker at the Treasury Building and the tunnel leading there from the White House. The tunnel was constructed during World War II and was totally deserted. Along the way were many closed and locked rooms labeled 'Cot Room # xx, for use by support people in the event of an attack. The rooms probably hadn't been opened since they were constructed and were stocked with bottled water and k-rations in the 1940s. There were no keys to the rooms. Matt said to Benson in a sharp tone he rarely used. "Get the Army Corps of Engineers in here and open the doors. Got it?"

Benson, not used to such authoritative talk, did just that. It is amazing how quickly they can respond. In an hour, the first door was opened. Nothing. So they asked Matt what to do, and he responded as if they were a bunch of children, "Look at the handles. They are covered with 50 years of dust and dirt."

The engineers did as ordered and discovered one with no dust or dirt. They opened that door, and voila! There was the First Lady and the Secret Service agent.

Matt said, "Give me a few minutes with them."

If you have never seen Dr. Matt Miller, you should know that he is tall, slender, deeply tanned from golfing, and he speaks with a calm reassuring tone that makes a person respect him.

"We've been looking for you," said Matt. "A few people were getting worried. How did you get in here?"

"I had a key from World War II in the 1940s," replied the Secret Service agent. "Several of us were stationed here. I know I don't look that old, but I am."

"Next Ma'am, why are you here?" asked Matt. "I won't tell anyone. It's only between you and me. But, don't worry. I'll fix things up for you."

"I just have this awful flu and look at me," said the First Lady. "I look like a witch. I'm blubbering all over the place. I've been crying, and my hair is a total mess."

Matt said to the Secret Service agent, "Why did you do it?"

"Because she asked me to. That's my job," was the answer. "I am required to do what the First Lady desires."

Matt went out of the cot room, and asked Benson to call the President. "Tell him that the First Lady has been found and to come to cot room #37 with her raincoat and a rain hat. Pronto!"

The President arrived in less than 10 minutes, and Matt said, "Be kind to her, Mr. President, she needs you now."

Matt and the General met with the President in his private office. "Thank you, gentlemen," said the President. "You've solved my crisis, and I will be eternally grateful. Please send me a bill for whatever amount you please."

"There is no need Mr. President," said the General. "Our work is gratis."

On the way home in the White House jet, both Matt and the General were very pleased. Matt said, "That certainly was a worthwhile trip."

"It was indeed," said the General.

"I could use a good round of golf," said Matt. "Sounds good to me," answered the General.

Life is good.

And this was the way it was.

END OF CHAPTER THREE AND PART 1

Part 2

THINGS START TO CHANGE

Chapter 4

CHANGE IS INEVITABLE

The phone rang at 8 pm and the housekeeper answered. All the caller said rather distinctly was, "General Miller."

"Just a minute, please," said the housekeeper, rather irritated. She was used to a more pleasant manner. "I'll see if he is available."

"If he isn't," continued the caller. "Find him on the double."

The housekeeper walked upstairs, as slowly as she could and entered the General's private study.

"There is a call for you, Sir," said the housekeeper. "The caller was very rude. I should have hung up on him."

"I'll take it," said the General.

It was the call the General did not want to hear. He knew it would happen someday.

"Miller here," said the General.

"General, you are ordered to report to the Pentagon tomorrow at no later than 2 pm," said the caller. "Dress uniform is required. A military jet will pick you up at 10 am. If you are not available or cannot be available, you know who to call. Bring military credentials. This call is finished. Your operator was very curt."

"We respond in turn," said the General before he hung up.

The General sat back in his chair. It was the call he had dreaded for more years than he could imagine. A position as a U.S. military general officer is a lifetime position. The individual must report for duty as ordered. The only exception us if a person is disabled and that condition had been recorded previously.

"I've been called back to duty," said the General. "Please press my dress uniform and place thereon my insignia. I will give my shoes a good polish. Do you know where the polishing kit is located?"

"I'm sorry to hear that, Sir," said the housekeeper. "Your polishing kit is on the floor of the closet, at the rear. Will I lose my position?"

"No, not at all," replied the General. "All activities will proceed as before. I fact, you will have a significant pay raise because you will have additional responsibility. From now on, if a I get a call, just say I am not available. I will inform Matt, Ashley, and Anna. I will keep you informed. You are the best employee I have ever had."

The housekeeper smiled. It was what she had hoped for.

Matt and Ashley had just started a movie and the popcorn was still hot when Matt's satellite phone rang.

"Matt here," answered Matt. He knew the call was from the General.

He knew intuitively that the call was important. The General usually called at 6 am, so this was a serious phone call.

"I've been called back to active duty," said the General. "I report tomorrow. They will pick me up at the local airport at 10 am, Dress uniform. No other information."

"I'm sorry, Sir," replied Matt. "I'll take you to the airport. We will pick you up at 9:30. Can I do anything to help you, and can you tell me why you were called back to duty?"

"Don't know anything," answered the General. "Probably some O7 or O8 said to the press that we would be in a war with China, or some other country in two years."

"Okay, I'll see you tomorrow, and we will talk on the way," said Matt as he terminated the satellite call.

Matt had his phone on speaker, so Ashley heard everything.

"What is an O7 or O8?" asked Ashley.

"It is a Brigadier or Major General," said Matt. "The General was an O9, and he was promoted to an O10 for service while retired. The General is a big deal in the military, so it is probably an important situation. We may never find out why he was recalled. It is normally top secret."

"Let's give it a try, that is the movie," continued Matt. "The popcorn is still warm."

"Why do they refer to the general as O7 or O8, for example?" asked Ashley. "I know that I just asked you this."

In combat, they put the insignia on the front of the uniform so an enemy sniper doesn't know what kind of officer they are," answered Matt. "It's 'better to shoot an O8 then an O5, for example. When the insignia is on the front, the enemy can't easily tell."

"Now I know," said Ashley. "How do you know that kind of stuff?"

"I just remember things on TV and the newspaper," said Matt. "I learned to observe things when I was a student."

"Okay, let's watch the movie."

END OF CHAPTER FOUR

Chapter 5

A PERSONAL PROBLEM EMERGES

The next morning, Matt rose early, did his ablutions, and brought a cup of fresh coffee to Ashley.

"You're up early," said Ashley. "This business with the General must have you worried."

"It does, I have to admit," replied Matt. "Everything is a secret, and a person never knows what is going to happen. He might end up in some foreign location leaded with danger. Probably not, but you never know."

"He's probably going to be there to baby sit the young generals." chided Ashley. "Those O10s just sit in meetings and enjoy a bit of golf. There is a course on every base."

"You may be right, and I hope you are," said Matt. "But it does upset our extra-curricular activities for a while.""

"I don't think it works that way," said Ashley. "I think it opens up new possibilities."

"That's another one of those famous Ashley's laws of behavior," said Matt. "We'll see. Maybe the General is truly holding us back. Then on the other hand, perhaps we are better off being held back. Do you want to come with me when I take the General to the airport?"

"Do you think he would mind?" asked Ashley.

"No he wouldn't," answered Matt. "He likes you. He thinks you are a quiet genius, and so do I."

So Matt and Ashley left for the General's house in Matt's Porsche Taycan electric car."

Matt and Ashley arrived at the General's mansion fifteen minutes early, and the General was on the covered porch ready to go.

He took one look at the Porsche and said, "We're not going in that car. It's way too fancy. Let's take my car."

"Your car is a Tesla S EV that stands for Electric Vehicle," replied Matt. "It is just as expensive."

"People don't know it, so let's get going," said the General.

Ashley looked over at Matt. He was really irritated. Matt rarely was irritated.

At the airport, the jet was waiting with its fan jet engines running. The General was helped up and in, and the aircraft was off. The airport that had been closed for the operation opened up like nothing had happened.

After the General boarded the airplane, Ashley looked over at Matt again, as if to ask what bothered him,

"We are out here to facilitate his recall," said Matt. "We don't have to be here. He could be a little nice. He isn't back in the service yet. Even there, they will not put up with him."

"Would you like to go to Starbuck's?" asked Matt. "I could enjoy a tasty scone."

"Which one," asked Ashley.

"Do you mean which scone or which Starbuck's?" asked Matt.

"You know I mean which Starbuck's," said Ashley. "You're trying to bug me. Now you're the one that irritating"

"Sorry, you know that I mean the old one," said Matt. "The new one is open air and everyone is looking around to see who is there."

"That is just intellectual curiosity," replied Ashley.

"Yeah right," said Matt. "We've had some good conversations there. I can't explain it."

"The macchiatos are good and the seats are well placed so a couple of people can have a conversation without having 80 million people looking at you and wondering what secret you are discussing," said Ashley.

"You are probably right there," said Matt. "Maybe, that's the reason that libraries are so good for study. No one is talking, and not too many are looking."

"I'm buying," said Ashley. "Beat you to it."

"I'll get a seat," said Matt. "I think our window seat is free."

Ashley came back with two venti macchiatos and two scones, and up walked Harry Steevens, Matt's old math buddy, and occasional helper with some of the General's problems.

"I see you two are not on a diet," said Harry. "How are you guys? I was just in the area and decided to come in to see if you guys were in here.""

"We're okay," replied Matt. "The General just got called up. How are you, Harry?"

"Well, I would say I could be better, but I doubt I could be worse."

"Sounds bad," replied Ashley, "Is it you or someone else?"

"Actually, it is someone else, but at this exact moment, I'm the one that's feeling pretty lousy."

"Out with it," interjected Matt.

"My sister died," said Harry. "I thought they had her fixed up, but the process was so demanding that her whole body failed. Do you remember her?"

"I never met her, but her husband was my thesis advisor, as well as Harp Thomas' thesis advisor" said Matt.

"Have a seat Harry," continued Matt. "We will get you some coffee until you settle down. You don't look so good."

Ashley got up to get Harry some coffee, and Harry shuffled to the table and sat down.

END OF CHAPTER FIVE

SOMETHING HAPPENED

Ashley came back with a grandi coffee with cream and sweetener.

"What happened, Harry?" Ashley asked.

"My sister Katarina, who we and others call Kat, had this terrible inherited condition, and we had to go to the medical university to get assistance," said Harry. "The doctor there was A number one, even though the experimental medical medicine to sustain her was $4,000 a week. Since it was an experimental collage of drugs, an appropriate organization paid the cost. The medicine was so strong that it damaged her liver and kidneys, and affected her heart. She was married to that professor Kacan that we had in some math class. They were married for over 60 years, and I would say he is pretty distraught just about now."

"He was my thesis advisor as well as Harp Thomas', as I said," said Matt. "That is really sad. I suppose that we should visit him."

"I was going today," said Harry. "Their lifelong dream was to have a beach home, and they recently moved in. I have never even been there."

"I think you should go, Matt," said Ashley. "I'll go with you if you want. I know you don't like to do things like this."

"Otherwise, how are you personally, Harry," asked Matt.

"Not so good," answered Harry. "Several of our New Jersey officers have been called up because of some sort of crisis, so New Jersey that loaned me to Hilton Head called me back."

"Do you still carry that baretta on your ankle?" asked Ashley.

"I do," said Harry. "I haven't shot it for at least 6 months."

"I bet that was interesting," replied Matt.

"Well, not exactly," said Harry. "One of our residents had a rabid racoon in her yard, and I had to take care of it. If a racoon comes out during the day, it's rabid."

"Can I get you another coffee and a scone?" said Ashley.

"I guess I could use one," replied Harry.

"What would you like this time," asked Ashley. "I'm buying all day; I got a royalty check."

"Whatever," said Harry. "I haven't been to Starbuck's in years."

"I'll get you a venti macchiato and a blueberry scone," said Ashley. "Is that good with you?"

"Thanks for thinking of me," said Harry.

"Back to Dr. Kacan," continued Matt. "I haven't seen or talked to him in a few years. He was my best buddy, even though he was my advisor. His complete name was Gregory Kacan. He was as pleasant as any other person I've known. He once told me he spent all of his time with his wife, outside of his university work. They thought the same on just about everything. He said he loved to go shopping with her. I remember her name Katarina and he called her Kat. She liked the phrase, 'Kat on the Beach'. She was a good shopper and he tagged along behind her – like at Christmas time. When they got to the cashier, she would meekly say, 'Are you paying'?"

Ashley came back with the macchiato scone and Harry said, "This is good. How much did it cost?"

"I don't know," answered Ashley. "I used a credit card. I don't carry money anymore."

"I don't either," said Matt. "There is not a cent on my person. Times have really changed."

Matt and Harry made a plan of a sorts. Harry would go that day, and then Matt would visit Dr. Kacan afterwards.

Harry Steevens left for Gregory Kacan's beach home, after agreeing with Matt to have his visit in two days exactly. Dr. Kacan probably will be looking forward to it.

END OF CHAPTER SIX AND PART TWO

Part 3

BACKGROUND INFORMATION

Chapter 7

GREG AND KAT

Greg and Kat met in college and lived a good life. Actually, they were together in a course only once. In that one course, they sat in the same row in the classroom and the student, who sat between them, said to Kat that Greg was going to ask her for a date. Kat was one of those students that took down every word that the professor said. Greg, a math student, just sat there and listened and watched. Kat thought he was some kind of dunce and was not at all interested. On the first and succeeding exams, Greg earned a better score than Kat and as expected, Greg did ask Kat for a date, and the rest is history. Well, not quite.

Greg commonly explained that in math courses, the professor described methods, problems, and mathematical proofs wherein every little squiggle meant something. A good math student observes everything exactly as the professor writes on the board each letter, number, and the so-called squiggle, as mentioned. Accordingly, it is the students job to write down the important symbols in class and later copies his or her notes and subsequently – like that day or night – does the assigned problem sets. The good student misses nothing. So that is how a good math student can be also good in other subjects. There might be other techniques, of course, but the situation of Greg and Kat is a simple example.

Greg and Kat had similar backgrounds, although different in detail. Both were depression kids, so they were not poor, but never had very much spending money. Greg's father had the same job for almost 50 years and had yearly vacations and a solid family life. Kat's father changed jobs and the family was frequently on the road from one job site to another. Kat always laughed when the situation of rest stops came up. The problem was, as most people know, that people are different. When asked by her mother, Kat would reply 'I didn't have to go but I went'. However, both fathers and mothers, of course, were active in church and social affairs. Greg's parents had good jobs and started off well. They bought a nice house, stylish car, and had interesting friends.

When Greg was born, their life changed a lot, and not for the better. Kat's parents had a rough time of it, together with medical conditions. To sum up, both Greg and Kat needed someone to be nice so to speak, and they found each other.

Greg and Kat were an exceptionally good team and obtained an exceedingly good life style of work, travel, and entertainment. Both relied on each other and were married for 63 years. They depended on each other for the smallest and largest things.

Then things changed. Kat came down with a serious inherited and incurable blood disease that necessitated experimental medicine and visits to the state's medical university. The procedure was successful but drained her physical system to the extent that she died recently. She was cremated and placed an appropriate facility. The individual facility had space for two persons. The facility was completely appropriate for individuals of Greg and Kat's caliber.

During their lifetime together, Greg and Kat were close to one another in every imaginable way: thinking, behavior, likes and dislikes, and dependencies. In short, two persons lived as one.

As their lives progressed, their mutual dependencies increased.

END OF CHAPTER SEVEN

Chapter 8

THE BEACH HOME

During Kat's sickness, the couple purchased a beach house. Greg had been a successful professor and benefitted from Kat's typing and a good academic atmosphere. Kat was cremated and interred in a storage facility. Kat worked as a librarian at first but then settled down to taking care of the kids, typing her husband's books, and enjoying activities in a quilting group in which she was the star quilter.

They had wanted a beach home for years, and Greg had written several fictional books classed as 'beach reads'.

Greg and Kat were very close. Kat was cremated and interred in a storage facility with room for Greg, when the time occurred.

After Kat's death, Greg visited her every day and told her of all current events, wishes, and desires. Greg benefitted greatly from the visits, as he was terribly lonesome.

With a scientific background, Greg did not believe in an afterlife from an academic perspective. Personally, however, he could not believe that life to some extent did not exist after physical death. Greg deeply believed that someday, modern science would come up with a progressive form of afterlife.

Greg and Kat's beach house – or should be say home – was a total success. They enjoyed the warm atmosphere with cool breezes, the sound of waves crashing against the levy, the nasty rain storms, and for the unique ability to take long walks in the soft white sand. There weren't many people around and that in itself was a definite blessing.

At first, Kat's inherited sickness was in complete control and Greg enjoyed his activities, such as his new found hobby of fiction writing. It gave him creative opportunities that he never had before.

Kat formed a special quilting group that they named themselves as the Fab Five, since it was comprised of five quilters. The five quilters was an ambitious group of avid quilters that met every Wednesday to discuss whatever quilters discuss, such as challenges and to help each other win difficult tasks. Greg believed they liked to meet because the atmosphere was good, as were Kat's snacks and other beautiful edibles.

The girls in the Fab Five helped each other and gave suggestions, but the conversation was the main activity, because there was always too much to say and not enough time to say them. Greg was popular as he loved to eat and didn't mind an occasional heavy lifting.

As Kat's disease progressed, Greg gradually took over the daily chores giving Kat more time for quilting. But even that took its toll on Kat's quilting.

Eventually, the powerful medicines that Kat had to take took its tole on Kat's other systems and Kat gradually passed on to another life.

As one could imagine, after 63 years of married life, the resultant loneliness on Greg's part was enormous. He promised to visit Kat at least once every day, and he truly honored his commitment.

END OF CHAPTER EIGHT

Chapter 9

THE FIRST VISITOR

Harry Steevens knocked on the door of Greg and Kat's beautiful beach home. Greg came to the door, and for a second or two, didn't recognize who Harry was.

"It's your long lost brother-in-law," said Harry. "I just came to see how you were."

"You missed the ceremony for Kat," said Greg. "I was really mad at you. It's okay though, I'm sure you had a good reason. You have a good character."

"I was out of the country bringing a prisoner back," said Harry. "When a person is in law enforcement, your life is not your own. I loved Kat and still do. I think you chose the best wife in the world, and she chose the best husband. You were a team."

"Thanks, Harry," said Greg. "Kat always spoke highly of you.

You were a good brother when you were kids and things got tough. She always said you were the brains of the family. I remember when you graduated and got an A in all of your math courses. The only other person to do that was Matt Miller. What ever happened to you?"

"I was a kid," said Harry. "I skipped two years of school; one in grammar school and the other in high school. I didn't have the right perspective. If I could do it over, I would have continued with math and tried to get a PhD. That's the way life is. You gain some and you lose some. Matt wants to visit you. Maybe in a couple of days."

"How is he doing?" asked Greg. "I haven't heard from him in a while."

"He's doing well," answered Harry. "He teaches math and works with his grandfather on projects for the government. His wife works with them. Matt is the big brain."

"Did you hear that?" asked Greg. "It was someone talking. It sounded like 'Hello' and 'I can help you'.

"I didn't hear anything," said Harry. "I think my ears are pretty good. I have to take a physical every year. This state we live in is the most conscientious state in the country."

"There it goes again," said Greg. "Someone is talking to us."

"Maybe it is someone outside," replied Harry. "You're on the beach. When you're on the beach, you never know."

"You're probably right," said Greg. "I probably just want to hear something."

"I have to hit the road," said Harry. "I'm on duty in 15 minutes."

"Thanks for visiting," said Greg. "It has helped me a lot. I'm pretty lonesome."

Harry left and Greg made himself a ham sandwich with chips and a can of soda, and turned on the wide screen TV.

END OF CHAPTER NINE AND PART THREE

Part 4

THE PLOT THICKENS

ANOTHER VISITOR TO THE BEACH HOUSE

Greg and Kat had been married for a very long time. Longer than most persons would ever think it were possible. As mentioned, they did everything together. In fact, they functioned as a single human entity. Every form of activity was performed with others knowledge. Most functions were preformed with the other's knowledge and approval. Otherwise, it was not performed.

After her death, Greg spent a lot of time talking to Kat, even though it was clearly obvious she was not there and would not be answering. A lot of Greg's speech was simply habitually inclined. Every interaction, as in 'hi, I'm home', was performed as it was in the past. If something good happened, Greg would inform Kat, and the same when bad consequences occurred. It was obviously a one way conversation, but it did not seem to matter. Greg was conversing with the spouse he truly loved, now and was forever. Then on one calm and peaceful day, something changed.

Greg pulled up in front of the beach home. He had done some everyday chores and entered the house; he was lonesome, tired, and frustrated. He did not sleep well the previous night. Greg truly missed Kat and his grief was stronger than usual.

As Greg opened the door, he said to Kat, "I'm back. I wish you were with me. The traffic was terrible."

Greg received a reply, "Hello, I can help you." Greg was puzzled. 'Am I hearing things', he said to himself. He looked around the entrance way. No one was there. He went through the family room and into the kitchen. No one.

"I'm here, but you can't see me. I can help you. I died just like your wife Kat. I am lonesome and frustrated, just like you are, except that I am not alive."

The voice continued.

"I am near you," said the voice. "I am all over; in front of you; behind you; above you. I don't know where I am. All I know is that you talked to me, and I replied."

"Why are you talking to me?" asked Greg.

"I try to carry on a conversation with any person that is alive and talks to me," said the voice. "I can tell if a person is alive or not alive."

"Actually, I have not been able to talk to anyone that is not alive," continued the voice. "You are the first. In my life, I was a scientist and I try to figure things out. I'm trying to test if two persons like myself can talk to one another."

"How long will you talk to me?" asked Greg.

"I'm also trying to figure that out also," said the voice. "I don't know how long I can correspond, period. To anyone. I do not even know what I look like."

"You must be pretty small, if I can't see you," replied Greg.

"There are useful things in normal life that are small, such as atoms, neurons, protons, neutrinos, and others," said the voice. "It is possible that everyone who dies ends up that way. Actually, I can tell if I am talking to a person like myself, or I am talking to a person that is alive. Let's call me an *ope*. Ope is a *hope* without the h. I am hoping that is true. That is where 'hope' comes from."6

"Now, every person that dies is transformed – so to speak – into an ope," continued the voice. "But all opes are not the same. *Now, I'm guessing, because I do not have full senses, as you do. When a person dies, a transformation results. The cells in a person continue to live – maybe exist – for a certain amount of time. Like 12 days, or 3 days, or whatever. During that time, nature generates an ope that just exists and does not communicate or one that does. Now here is what I am almost sure of. Initially, a new ope communicates or it does not. I am not saying they can communicate or not. Maybe the number of days the cells live is not the same. If there is communication, let us say, communicates to them, then the days the ope exists longer and it is also a mechanism to communicate. If and how they can actually talk us an open item, at least for the moment. But if there is no communication with them, they are still alive but all they do is exist in the abstract form I am calling an ope without communication capacity."*

The voice continues, "Perhaps they are blown around like a neutron or a neutrino, or some other particle. Just like other particles, there are billions or trillions of opes floating around.

"Aren't you getting tired of talking?" asked Greg.

"No, I do not feel tired, but I do wonder about maybe using up all of my capacity to do so,"

said the voice. "I'll talk to you again in a few days. I have to do some thinking."

The voice named *ope* stopped talking and Greg made himself a ham sandwich with chips and two cans of soda, and turned on the wide screen TV.

END OF CHAPTER TEN

HARRY AND MATT
GET TOGETHER

Harry Steevens left Greg's house, checked in online to his assignment for the day, and headed out to a day of traffic enforcement on the New Jersey turnpike, as usual. He wished he were back in Hilton Head doing something interesting. He stuck with the New Jersey State Police because he had seniority and a good 401K plan.

Matt was home in his study apparently looking up something online, which was unusual for him. He like to keep hands dirty, as they called the age old mathematical practice of using paper and a pencil or ballpen to prove theorems and develop mathematical theories on new things like string theory.

Ashley, just a few feet away, was fussing with the corner of a quilt. They were at home.

"Looks like you are having some difficulty," said Matt sympathetically.

"I am," said Ashley. "I'm trying to learn how to MITRE a corner. Do you have any idea of what that might be?"

"Sorry, quilting is too darn complicated for me," replied Matt. "Why don't you call one of your Fab Five and bribe her with a trip to Starbucks. I have a taste for a caramel macchiato and a scone."

"What about Millie," said Ashley. "She lou ikes you and always gives you an enormous American hug."

"That's because she's bigger than I am."

"She likes you because you are nice to her," said Ashley. "She has trouble at home. Her husband too much money on horses, and her son and his wife bought their house from them, and they want the master bedroom. I think she would be the best because she knows the most about quilting."

"What are you working on to change the subject," continued Ashley. "You usually are fiddling around with paper and pen, and now you are looking things up on the Internet."

"There is a new subject in mathematics called *reverse mathematics*," said Matt. "Funny thing that's the same name that the General made up when he helped fix up those P-51s during the war. He just made up that name, because all important things have names."

"So, what is the real reverse mathematics?", asked Ashley.

"Usually, you use axioms to prove theorems, but with reverse mathematics you start out with theorems, and figure out the necessary axioms," answered Matt. "I don't know much more. They are going to have a conference on it in Zürich Switzerland at ETH."

"When," lit up Ashley. "Do you want to go? We could have breakfast at Sprungli and dinner at the Zeughauskeller restaurant."

"I don't know enough to go," said Matt.

"Then learn," replied Ashley.

"So why don't you ask your PhD advisor," continued Ashley. "You always said he was a quick study and he has plenty of time, since his wife died. Weren't you going to visit him. I thought you and he were kind of buddies."

"I'm waiting to see him after I talk to Harry, who visited him," said Matt. "He's on duty today. I'm a little nervous about it. I don't know what to say to someone when their spouse dies."

"Just say you are sorry and you noted how the two of them did things together," said Ashley. "The important thing is that you say something. Like when somebody's husband dies, you say 'He was a good husband and a very kind man'."

The visit to Starbucks with Millie was enjoyable. Millie gave Matt a big hug and was a barrel of fun. Millie was glad to be with people that appreciated her.

As one could predict, the subject of Matt's buddy Greg came up. Millie came from a large family that had legs into almost every subject known to man. At least that is what they thought. Millie stated that in the case of a man and a woman in a long marriage with a close relationship and the woman dies, then the man is affected greatly on the subjects of loneliness, organization, and unaccompanied conversation. They talked a lot to no one.

Matt and Ashley liked Millie. It was unique to observe two highly educated people listen extraordinarily close to a relatively uneducated woman.

Matt got together with Harry toward the end of the day when Harry was off shift. Matt secured a good table in the General's Green Room restaurant. Matt offered a prime filet to Harry who turned in down in favor of a tilapia fish dinner. Harry didn't have much to say.

"He didn't talk to me very much, except to exchange pleasantries," said Harry. "The problem was that Greg got into a conversation with someone else and there was no one for me to converse with. He talked at great length with someone, but I am sorry to say, I could not determine who he was talking to. It wasn't like a dream, but rather a give and take conversation in which the other person was running the conversation. It was like the other person was telling Greg something. It was a weird conversation. There was no other person and only Greg was talking. When you visit with him, record the conversation secretly on your call phone. Perhaps you can make something out of it. I don't feel like visiting Greg again."

After that statement, Matt, Ashley, and Harry had a pleasant dinner. They were all roughly the same age and the conversation bounced between subjects in a friendly manner.

A husband and wife in a nearby table observed the group with great interest. The woman said, "They certainly are different. The manner of discussing things was so informal and they laughed a lot. The big boss sure puts a damper on thongs like laughing and having a good time." Her husband replied, "Age sure makes a difference in how things are done. Americans are certainly like other people in the world."

END OF CHAPTER ELEVEN

Chapter 12

GREG AND MATT GET TOGETHER

Matt decided to visit Greg and did not want to go alone. Ashley refused for the same reason. Actually, Matt did not want to go at all. Matt decided that after lunch would be best.

Matt drove to Greg and Kat's beach house and parked in front. He went to the front door and it was partially open. No one answered. He looked to the side and Greg's car was there. Matt went back to his car and waited 30 minutes. He went back up and Greg was there.

"Hi Matt," said Greg. "It's good to see you. Were you here long? If so, I guess I didn't hear you. I was talking to someone. Hold on a minute, I have to finish the conversation. Come into the family room with me. I won't be a minute."

Matt turned on his cell phone, sat down, and started recording. The minute turned into an hour and Matt was totally bored.

The conversation centered around the problem of how Greg could talk to Kat. Kat had died and was cremated. Assuming that an afterlife exists, they had to find out where she was and then turn her on, so to speak, so they could converse. That information Matt could deduce from the conversation. Only Greg seemed to be talking.

They didn't know if Kat had the capability for speech and if so, was it turned on or how to turn it on?

The voice that Greg was talking to was under the opinion that Kat was an *ope*, and would not be able to speak to Greg unless the voice – they started to call her an *ope* – turned the *ope* on. When she died, her capability for conversation was not available or turned on and the voice thought he could do it. This information Matt was able to deduce from the conversation.

Next, they didn't know where the Kat *ope* was. Assuming she was a particle in the form of an org of some sort, maybe the wind or the gravitational force of another planet carried her away.

Assuming that Kat's *ope* was nearby where she was interred, the question was how to get the voice *ope* to where the Kat *ope* was.

The voice *ope* could not propel itself but was somehow attracted to Greg. They discussed that for a good 15 minutes. They figured out a method by which the voice *ope* could trail Greg to the place of interment.

Matt was amazed. The level of creativity was huge.

The big question turned out to be how would they recognize the Kat *ope* when they found her.

Matt noticed that it was not a normal human-to-human conversation. Many of the remark were entangled as if they were coming from the same person. It was like Greg's brain was talking and then told him what to hear. I short, Greg was answering his own speech. It seemed as though Greg's brain was telling itself and Greg didn't know it.

Then in a flash, Matt had it. Greg's brain was commanding him. It was like when a soldier was in combat, there was someone giving orders, but that person was itself.

Matt turned off his recorder, he had enough. This was a job for the intelligence community.

The conversation ended, and Greg was seemingly back to his normal self. From Matt's point of view, they needed to consult with someone, and he knew who that person was.

Greg was fine and agreed to make a quick study on reverse mathematics and give a paper in Zürich. Greg said he didn't have enough money to travel to Switzerland, and Matt offered to pay from his budget. It was a white lie; faculty members don't normally have budgets and Matt decided that he or the General would cover Greg's expenses.

Matt offered to give some references, and Greg was overjoyed to be back into mathematics research. Matt said he would provide printouts of the papers to Greg and advise him of the conference and travel arrangements.

When Matt left Greg and Kat's house, he was totally happy. As far as he was concerned, he had the start of a solution. He sang a song on the drive home and had a laugh at himself.

When Matt got home, he burst in the door.

"You look happy," said Ashley. "He wasn't home."

"No, he was home and I had the experience of a lifetime," replied matt. "I have it all recorded, and I have an idea of what is going on. And, I might have a solution to his problem."

"That's good," said Ashley. "What would you enjoy for dinner? You can have fish or you can have fish. Otherwise, we have to go to your favorite Starbucks."

"How about the Green Room?" asked Matt.

"I could force myself," said Ashley.

END OF CHAPTERR TWELVE AND PART FOUR

Part 5

THE SEARCH FOR A SOLUTION

Chapter 13

DEVISING A PLAN

Matt and Ashley pulled up in front of the Green Room restaurant and got out of the car right outside of the entrance. There was no sign of any kind. There used to be a valet service, but the General fired the whole bunch of them as they dented his new Mercedes car.

"You can't park here," warned Ashley. They will tow you away or give you a ticket."

"It doesn't say no parking; anyway, I'm not parking," said Matt.

"You are and you know it," said Ashley.

"Listen," said Matt. "If I were parking, I would be in the parking lot behind the building. I'm not back there, so I am not parking."

"Then, what are you doing, smartie pants?" laughed Ashley. "You'll get a ticket or be towed away, like I said."

"I'm not parking as I said, and if I were, I would be in the lot," said Matt with a smile on his face. "The guard or whatever he is will say I'm parking and I'll say I'm not parking because I am not in the parking lot. He will be bewildered and just walk away."

"Nobody is that stupid," said Ashley.

"Wait and see," answered Matt.

"You will be walking home smartie pants," said Ashley. "Wait and see yourself."

Matt and Ashley were in a good mood.

The maître d noticed them and gave them the best table in the house, next to our rich friends that happened to be there most of the time. The waiters hated them because they gave a tip of 50 cents for each person. The frequently returned food for one reason or another. Ashley put her purse on the table to block the conversation. They both ordered tilapia fish, chips, and a soft drink.

"Now that we are all settled down for a juicy conversation," said Ashley. "What is the story on Greg Kacan and his former wife Katarina Stevens who is the sister of Harry Steevens, who changed his last name for an unknown reason and carries a beretta on his ankle."

"Wow, that is some sentence," said Matt. "You ought to copyright that one. Well, here is the story in a nutshell. You would think Greg is as nutty as a fruitcake, but I'm sure that he is not. Pure and simple, he talks to himself. There is no one talking to him. He is talking to himself and answering out loud. When he is listening to himself, there is no sound. It is in his brain. It would sound more plausible if I used the word *mind* instead of *brain*. I have recorded everything. You can tell this from his speech pattern and choice of words. His speech sounds like he is answering to someone that is giving him information or a command of some sort. Only, he can hear the command, because it is only in his mind all by itself."

"Well, I'll be," said Ashley.

"Hey, that's my line," said Matt.

"Okay, you can have it back," answered Ashley.

"Maybe the government intelligence people are involved," said Matt. "This is a job for the General. Maybe they are training agents or soldiers to command themselves. Let's call it the **Unicom Project**, where the 'Uni" refers to 'only one' person. All government projects have a name, at least that is the way it is in movies."

"I bet you are going to call Kimberly," said Ashley.

"I am and also the General," said Matt. "Get your Army uniform ready. I believe you were a Major."

"And you a full Colonel," replied Ashley.

They both finished their fish and hurried out of the restaurant. Matt left a $100 bill to cover the meal and the tip. The waiter had a big smile. He loved those beautiful and rich people.

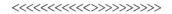

The nosey people were bewildered. "You haven't said anything this time," said the husband. 'You are totally surprised and so am I."

END OF CHAPTER THIRTEEN

Chapter 14

ARRANGEMENT IN THE PENTAGON

Matt called Kimberly first, since she was easy to reach and almost always on duty. Kimberly worked for the government in a secret location that housed a super computer with software that stored information on most things in the free and not free world.

"Hi Kimberly," said Matt. "How are you and how is your job hunting going?"

"The management get wind of it and made me a big offer, a real big offer,: said Kimberly. "I got more money, a management job, and guaranteed employment, regardless of my behavior, for the rest of my working life plus twenty years. So I stopped looking and accepted. Also, I have a government car to be renewed every two years, and 4 weeks' vacation every year. Plus regular training education on the latest techniques, whether or not I use the information. Thanks for what you were going to do for me."

"I'm happy for you Kimberly," said Matt. "You deserve it."

"Okay, what's up?" asked Kimberly.

"We are looking at a man who ostensibly is talking to a person that has died. I heard, recorded, and studied the interactions and feel the person under investigation is producing the interaction between himself and himself."

"There was a project like that a few years ago called the Unicom Project that was cancelled by the Congress. Let me look it up," said Kimberly. "Yes, here it is. The idea is to have the brain give orders to itself, like a soldier in combat. The project had one participant and he didn't finish the program. The project received a five star rating. Do you want his name? Also, there are a few lines of information about him."

"I do," said Matt.

"His name was Gregory Kacan, and he was doing quite well. Received good reviews. We have nothing more on him."

"Well, I'll be," said Matt. "He was my PhD thesis advisor. We were good friends and people said we were buddies."

"Well. I'll be also," said Kimberly.

"That's it," said Matt.

"What's it?" replied Kimberly. "You will have to go to the Director of Intelligence to have his file opened and his tutor identified. Here's more. They were obviously concerned because he did not complete his training. They were concerned with or about him for some reason, but he completely disappeared."

"Were they concerned that be might do damage or hurt or kill someone?" asked Matt.

"He was not a security risk because he was not exposed to any U.S. secrets. He is not dangerous. I think they were worried that his personal life was jeopardized and he might not be able to hold a position. I mean a job, and be homeless, or something like that."

"We're on it now, Kimberly," said Matt. "We can handle it. Congratulations on your new position. You are valuable and still the best. Thank you."

"You're welcome, Matt," said Kimberly. "You are also the best."

Matt called the General and gave him the problem and the details. The General told Matt that he would have to come to the Pentagon. He, the General, would contact his friend Mark Clark, Director of Intelligence and former Chief of Staff, about who the contacts were. He, the General, would arrange for meeting with the contacts in the Government and provide whatever assistance was required. Matt asked about that and then General surprised Matt.

"Matt, I'm the king around here with my for stars. All I do is attend meetings and gove advice."

"What abut transportation?" asked Matt.

"I'll have a military jet pick you and Ashley up tomorrow at 8:00 am in your local airport," said the General. "As I said, I have power. I'll have a contact for you tomorrow. Plan on staying the night, but that might not be necessary. We have new quarters in the Pentagon for military staff."

"I'm so surprised," said Ashley. "This case unraveled so quickly."

"It's a surprise for me too," said Matt. "The country is on high alert for some reason, and everything gets done a lot more quickly than normal."

END OF CHAPTER FOURTEEN

Chapter 15

AT THE PENTAGON

General Miller, Colonel Miller, and Major Miller were escorted into General Hutchinson's spacious office complex. On the door, it read:

General Richard Hutchinson
MD, PhD, PsychD

Dr. Hutchinson had three busy secretaries, one officer manager, one heavy Colonel, and a Major, as his executive assistant. There was a meeting room, medical office, two laboratories, an operating room, and a private office for General Hutchinson. There were two lavatories and a large kitchen and eating area. There were desks, tables, chairs, filing cabinets, and several storage rooms. No one besides the General had a private office. There was soft drink and candy machines in the kitchen, as well as coffee facilities.

General Hutchinson introduced himself as a military officer,

81

but preferred to be called Dr. Hutchinson or simply Hutch, the Pentagon psychiatrist. He ran the total operation, and he was a 4-star general officer. The moment the two generals shook hands, a psychological bond was established between the two men. That is the way that the military works. The group had many ongoing secret projects that were designed to enhance the security of the United States That too is the way the military works.

Dr. Hutchinson knew of the **Unicom Project**, since he was the initiator of it. He was additionally the designer and the executor of the operation. They had only one subject and he was an officer that recently been commissioned as a second lieutenant. His name was Gregory Kacan, who had entered in Dr. Hutchinson's domain after graduating from college with an ROTC commission. ROTC commissioned officers had excellent military training through local programs.

"The project with Lieutenant Kacan was progressing in an excellent manner under the initial design considerations," said Dr. Hutchinson. "Here is a transcript that we have on file. Remember this is what someone wrote and is not an edited record. It is a work in progress:"

> *Officers are often in a position where by good military procedures, troops have to engage in complicated and dangerous operations.*

> *Officers are trained to operate in those dangerous situations to officers and the troops under his command.*

> *Officers that command troops know what to do but are frequently hesitant to do so.*

The officers must be told to do something that they already know they should do beforehand.

The Unicom Project is designed to assist the commander in commanding himself.

The officers know what they must do but are reluctant to do it.

Dr. Hutchinson continued. "Although the considerations tend to be slightly overlapping, the process centers around the fact that the officer should be trained to listen to his own judgment about what to do. He has to listen to himself when giving an order. The key point is that the officer must be capable of listening to himself when determining what to do, and operate as though someone were actually telling him to do so.

The process is manifested by the officer listening to a voice giving an order, and the voice is his own voice dispatching the order.

The officer will think that the voice is someone else and not himself. He will refer to this voice as an *ope* that exists outside of his own body. No actual speech is involved, but the officer will think that the order is in fact outside of himself and is talking to him.

Thus, the officer is trained to operate as though he is being ordered.

An outsider viewing the situation sees an officer talking and responding in normal fashion without an incoming command. In short, the subject appears to be talking to himself. In trial, it appears to operate successfully on test persons and situations."

"How is this phenomena turned on and off?" asked Matt. "Can the officer get out of this mode?"

"That's the problem," said Hutch, which colleagues called him. "In test, we were able to do it by changing the intellectual environment through an intellectual challenge. We need some more research in this area."

"I suspect the subject cannot do this by himself or herself," replied Matt.

"Exactly, that's a perfect assessment, Matt, even though you are not a military Colonel and you Ashley are not a Major officer," said Hutch with a smile on his face.

"How do you know, Hutch?" asked the General.

"You know that by the time we get to O10, we can figure out practically everything."

"Just like I've determined that you, Dr. Hutchinson, are not military, but a contractor."

"Let's have lunch people, and I'll let you go back home and solve your problem," said Hutch. "Did I mention that the *Unicom Project* was cancelled right after Lieutenant Kacan left the project and our budget was slashed by Congress."

The lunch is the new cafeteria for officers was magnificent, and the food was beyond belief.

After lunch, Dr. Hutchinson ordered a Marine One helicopter to Dulles air field and a military jet back to New Jersey.

On the jet from Dulles to New Jersey, Matt asked how he knew that Hutch was a contractor.

"That was easy," said the General. "He didn't have any badges, just like the one I have on the right front just below the belt line. It's my reward for my current good service. I've finished my duty and have been discharged."

The General put his finger to his lips to signal not to talk because it probably would be recorded.

On the way back from the local airport to the General's mansion, Ashley asked Matt how he planned to rid Gregory Kacan of his problem of talking and responding to the hypothetical voice to which he supposedly talked and responded.

Matt was quick to answer, "I think I will move on that Reverse Mathematics conference we discussed. I think Zürich would be a good place that is far enough away and on a new subject to break Gregory's condition. I'll call Harp when we get home."

"I got that from the conversation," said the General. "Do you anticipate giving your buddy Harp a little cash for his efforts?"

"I was thinking of that," said Matt. "Remember he is married to Kimberly Jobsen, your old competitor of a sorts."

Harry Katzan Jr.

The general came out with a grin, "I think $1,000,000 would be appropriate. Do you agree."

"We do," said Matt with a smile.

Ashley couldn't help but laugh to herself, little boys and their money.

END OF CHAPTER FIFTEEN AND PART FIVE

Part 6

BACK TO NORMAL

Chapter 16

TO ZÜRICH AND BACK

Matt called Greg and set up an appointment to discuss Reverse Mathematics at the possible conference in Zürich, Switzerland, a great place to have a conference. They agreed to meet at noon. When Matt and Ashley got there, Greg was watching TV and eating a ham sandwich with chips and three cans of soda.

Matt brought several Reverse Mathematics references and copies of papers. Matt asked Greg how long he would need to write a paper and learn enough about the subject matter to host the conference.

Greg said 4 weeks and Ashley could tell from Matt's face that he would prefer to have it sooner.

"I think there is one of those festivals going on in Switzerland in 4 weeks," said Ashley. "Matt and I have our own university work to deal with. How about 3?"

"Okay, so we're on," said Matt. I'll ask the administrator at my school to set us up as a sponsor and announce the conference. Maybe, we also need a journal on the subject of Reverse Mathematics with papers by the same people who presented at the conference. Everyone likes to get a paper in the first issue of a journal. I have to get going; I have work to do."

On the way to Starbucks for lunch, Matt called Harp Thomas, his buddy, at ETH in Zürich, the number one Mathematics university in the world. Harp was happy to set up a conference, especially about getting a $1,000,000 honorarium for his efforts. He also offered to make reservations at the Zum Storchen hotel for Greg, Matt, and Ashley.

"I think I'll write a paper also." Said Matt. "It is nice to have a paper in the first issue of a journal." "You already said that," replied Ashley.

"Yes, but I didn't say it to you," answered Matt.

END OF CHAPTER SIXTEEN

Chapter 17

SWITZERLAND

The General was happy to be relieved of his military service. He offered to arrange for the flight and schedule. The Captain and First Officer were pleased as well. They liked Switzerland, but it would difficult to find anyone that did not like Switzerland. The pilots knew the General would manage expensive lodging for them and also reservations at the top restaurants in Zürich, known for their excellent food and wine and beer.

During the week of the conference, Greg was nowhere to be found. What a state of affairs. Ashley was ranting all over the place, and Matt was getting nervous, but tried not to show it. All he said was, "He'll be here, don't worry." But he was worried. Then he finally said to Ashley, "How do we get involved in ridiculous junk like this?"

The Ashley said, "Don't worry, he'll be here. He's probably out in some field talking to that nutty voice of his that is supposedly talking to him."

Then, on the day of travel, Greg showed up. Neither, Matt nor Ashley said anything.

The conference was a great success. The paper were good. The people were good. And, the venue was good. As usual, Harp did an excellent job of setting it up and was exceedingly proud of himself. I fact, he also presented a paper himself and won the best paper award. The prize was that his paper would be first in the journal.

Most people agreed that the best part of the conference was the location. That was the saying about conferences: location, location, location.

The persons that gave papers wanted to know when the first issue of the journal would come out. Matt said 6 weeks, but he had no idea of how long things like that would take.

The general brought Anna, his wife, along to visit Klosters, a scenic resort area in the Swiss mountains. He owned a small villa there, across the street from the famous restaurant/hotel where the actress Deborah Kerr had a *stom tishe*, otherwise known as a permanent reserved table when she was in town. The name of the restaurant is the Chesa Grischuna where the General and Anna had a wonderful dinner. Greg, Matt, Ashley, Harp, and Kimberly ventured up to Klosters to have a dinner at the Chesa with them. Life is good.

On the return flight, everyone except the pilots slept like a bunch of babies. There were a lot of nice things to see and do in Zürich and Switzerland at large., so the visitors took good advantage of the opportunity.

Greg was his usual self during the entire business trip.

END OF CHAPTER SEVENTEEN

Chapter 18

HOME AT LAST

The day after they returned from Switzerland, Matt and Ashley slept in, had breakfast at Starbucks, and decided to visit Greg.

Matt and Ashley parked in front and looked the place over. The front door was open.

They walked into the family room, and Greg was standing in the middle of the room talking to the voice ope. Dr. Hutchinson was totally wrong and the effort turned out to be a complete waste.

Ashley said to Matt, "It looks like there is HOPE after all."

Matt didn't say anything for a few minutes. Then he said something that Ashley was surprised to hear.

"We learned something," said Matt. "We were not wrong; we experienced something that we never thought of."

"Well, get on with it," said Ashley. "You usually do not talk this way."

"Greg experienced a case he was involved with that was an attempt to affect nature," said Matt. "Greg graduated as a second lieutenant, and because of his intellect, was chosen for an experiment. It was a well thought out attempt to alter the way the brain operates. It is to change the way the brain commands itself. Greg was and is exceedingly intelligent. He almost immediately realized what they were going to attempt a brain transformation and bolted. He left the project and didn't leave a return address. He saw through it. What we are witnessing is a healthy expression of human grief. Greg is okay. From his performance in Zürich, he is better than before he retired. He is experiencing grief, and it will go away. Every person does it differently. The fact that Greg was happily married for 63 years and was a close teammate with Kat only made it worse. He will be okay. We just have to give him time."

"As they say," said Ashley. "Time solves all problems. It looks like there is HOPE after all."

END OF CHAPTER EIGHTEEN PART SIX AND THE BOOK

Thanks for reading the book.
The author.

About This Book

This is a book of fiction and is intended for the entertainment of the reader. The main characters as well as other characters and events are totally made up. The objective of the book is to please the readership, and not intended to give a point of view or other information.

Our daughters, Kathryn and Karen, helped with the book when necessary and I would like to mention some other family members that provided inspiration: Sara, Daniel, Leah, Matthew, Tom, Katie, and Meghan. Have you ever been mentioned in someone's book? I haven't and probably the same for you.

Thanks for reading the book. The book follows the usual procedure of no violence, no sex, and no bad language. It is accessible to readers of all ages.

One more thing: thanks to Martin Lopez, John Wood, and Pia Olsen for their continued support.

About The Author

Harry Katzan, Jr. is a professor who has written several books and many papers on computers and service, in addition to some novels. He has been a advisor to the executive board of a major bank and a general consultant on various disciplines. He and his wife have lived in Switzerland where he was a banking consultant and a visiting professor. He is an avid runner and has completed 94 marathons including Boston 13 times and New York 14 times. He holds bachelors, masters, and doctorate degrees.

Books By Harry Katzan, Jr.

Computers and Information Systems

Advanced Programming
APL Programming and Computer Techniques
APL Users Guide
Computer Organization and the System/370
A PL/I Approach to Programming Languages
Introduction to Programming Languages
Operating Systems
Information Technology
Computer Data Security
Introduction to Computer Science
Computer Systems Organization and Programming
Computer Data Management and Database Technology
Systems Design and Documentation
Microprogramming Primer
The IBM 5100 Portable Computer
Fortran 77
The Standard Data Encryption Algorithm
Introduction to Distributed Data Processing
Distributed Information Systems
Invitation to Pascal
Invitation to Forth
Microcomputer Graphics and Programming Techniques

Invitation to Ada
Invitation to Ada and Ada Reference Manual
Invitation to Mapper
Operating Systems (2nd Edition)
Local Area Networks
Invitation to MVS (with D. Tharayil)
Introduction to computers and Data Processing
Privacy, Identity, and Cloud Computing

Business and Management

Multinational Computer Systems
Office Automation
Management Support Systems
A Manager's Guide to Productivity, Quality
Circles, and Industrial Robots
Quality Circle Management
Service and Advanced Technology

Basic Research

Managing Uncertainty

Service Science

A Manager's Guide to Service Science
Foundations of Service Science
Service Science
Introduction to Service
Service Concepts for Management
A Collection of Service Essays
Hospitality and Service

Little Books

The Little Book of Artificial Intelligence
The Little Book of Service Management
The Little Book of Cybersecurity
The Little Book of Cloud Computing
The Little Book of Managing Uncertainty

Novels

The Mysterious Case of the Royal Baby
The Curious Case of the Royal Marriage
The Auspicious Case of the General and the Royal Family
A Case of Espionage
Shelter in Place
The Virus
The Pandemic
Life is Good
The Vaccine
A Tale of Discovery
The Terrorist Plot
An Untimely Situation
The Final Escape
Everything is Good
The Romeo Affair
Another Romeo Affair

Reprints

The Royal Baby
The Royal Marriage
The General and Royal Family
Espionage in Academia

A Shelter is Good
Pandemic Story
The Good Life
The Discovery
The Terrorists
An Unexpected Happening
Service Management
Cybersecurity
Managing Uncertainty
Here, There and Everywhere

Advanced Novels

The Day After the Night Before
The Journey of Matt and the General
Two Necessary Escapes
Escape

Trilogies and Duologies

The Magnificent Monarchy
Worldwide Trouble
Winning is Good
The Good Life and Discovery
Up, Down and Anywhere

END OF BOOKS BY HARRY KATZAN JR.

Printed in the United States
by Baker & Taylor Publisher Services